THE CAT
WITH IRON CLAWS

THE CAT
WITH IRON CLAWS

Catherine Fisher

Illustrated by
Nicola Robinson

Pont

Published in 2012 by Pont Books, an imprint of
Gomer Press, Llandysul, Ceredigion SA44 4JL

ISBN 978 1 84851 317 4

A CIP record for this title is available from the British Library.

This book is published with the financial support of the
Welsh Books Council.

Printed and bound in Wales at
Gomer Press, Llandysul, Ceredigion.

CONTENTS

1

The Great Enchantment

Along the dark road a chariot thundered.

It was golden, and it gleamed like the sun. Sparks flashed like lightning from its huge wheels as the driver lashed on his four black horses.

Coll watched it come.

He was crouched behind a rock at the side of the road, and he'd been waiting a long time. Now his legs were stiff and his hand was sore where he leaned on the gritty track.

He was sweaty with fear.

But still he waited.

The chariot charged down the hill. Coll held his breath until the horses were so close he could see the flicker of their wild eyes. Then he jumped up, and ran out.

He stood, arms folded, in the middle of the road.

The driver gave a great yell and dragged on the reins. The chariot skidded, and the horses reared up, neighing with fury, their hooves thrashing the air above Coll's head. Foam from their harness flew over him like snow.

He closed his eyes in terror.

The wheels screamed. Would they stop, or run him over?

Then there was silence, until the whip cracked in his face. His eyes snapped open.

'Are you mad?' the driver roared. 'Are you crazy? Are you trying to get your stupid self killed!'

Coll swallowed. 'No, Uncle,' he said. 'I just want you to teach me the Secret.'

The driver of the chariot was a tiny man. He drove standing up in the harness, his thin red beard bristling, his face narrow, with hooded eyes. Now he howled in anger.

'Not again!'

The howl of Gwythelyn the Dwarf was a terrible sound. Coll wanted to crumple up and hide. But he managed to stand still and look bold.

Gwythelyn threw the whip aside and pointed a skinny finger at his nephew. 'Now look, Coll. This has got to stop. You've nagged me at breakfast and

supper. You've hidden in my stable and nagged me when I've ridden in from the hunt. You've nagged me every time you've cleaned my sword or polished my boots. Don't you ever think about anything else?'

Coll shook his head. 'I want to learn. I want to know the Great Enchantment. Only you can teach it to me.'

Gwythelyn groaned. He glared down at the awkward figure on the road.

Coll was his sister's son. A brown-haired, brown-faced, twig-thin, scrawny boy with legs too long for his body. An irritating, stubborn, clever brat. Clever enough to bear the weight of the Secret? Well, Gwythelyn thought, there was only one way to find out. At least he might get some peace then.

'Get in,' he snapped, picking up the whip. 'And be careful.'

Coll grinned in delight. He ran round and put his hand on the chariot, then snatched it back with a yell. 'It's hot!'

'Of course it's hot, stupid. And don't go near the Beakers.'

Coll climbed on. As the horses were whipped up and the chariot jolted into speed he glanced curiously at the Beakers. There were three of them, strange vessels made of some bright metal. They had spouts for pouring and lids joined to their bodies with fine gold chains that swung as the chariot bumped over the road. They were locked in a brace to keep whatever was in them from spilling, and Coll was glad they were, because the heat that came off them was already scorching him.

He edged away.

The Beakers were famous. Every day Gwythelyn filled them in the east and drove with them into the west. They leaked a golden glow. Splashes from them seared the skin. They lit the Otherworld with a fiery heat and no one but Gwythelyn could open them without being consumed by flames. No one knew what was in them, but some people said it was the fuel that powered the sun.

By the time the chariot came to Gwythelyn's court Coll was sure all the one side of his face was burned and red. He jumped down quickly.

Gwythelyn leapt to the ground, leaving the horses to his steward.

'With me. Now.'

Coll ran through the hall, trying to keep up with the tiny man. Servants got out of the way quickly. Dogs sloped off. Everyone could see there was trouble in the air.

Gwythelyn led the way through the solar and the kitchens, up the private stair that twisted round and round, up and up to the stone room at the top of the tower. He unlocked the door with a bronze key and pushed Coll inside.

Once in, he locked the door again.

Coll stared round.

He'd never been in his uncle's secret room.

The walls were stone and hung with tapestries, each one showing strange animals, a hunting pack of white hounds, a man with antlers, a bubbling cauldron. There was a fire burning in a hearth in the centre of the room, and some books on a table. A harp stood in the corner. A locked chest stood under the window. Some berried branches were piled on the floor. And that was all.

Coll was a bit disappointed.

He had expected magic things, but this was like any other room.

Gwythelyn walked around him three times, looking him up and down. 'How old are you?'

'Fifteen, Uncle.'

'Old enough then. Can you read?'

'Yes, Uncle.'

'Can you write?'

'Yes, Uncle.'

'Can you use a sword, tame a horse, make a

poem? Do you know oak from ash, hawk from swallow? Can you throw a spear higher, run faster, play better at chess than any boy at court?'

'I can, Uncle.' And he could. He had practised all those things for years.

'Hmmm.' Gwythelyn frowned. In truth he had decided to teach Coll magic a long time ago. But he still wasn't sure the boy was ready. So all he said was: 'Magic is not easy. Magic costs. Listen to me now, and don't forget anything I tell you.'

He pulled Coll close to him.

And he whispered the Secret in his ear.

The Secret was ancient. It was one of the Three Great Enchantments of the Island of Britain. If you knew it you could change your shape. You could change the shape of others. You could recognise the enchanted ones. And you could remain unharmed by monsters and men.

Coll felt power spread through him like warmth from a fire. His eyes opened wide. 'It's wonderful!' he breathed.

'Yes. But be careful.' Gwythelyn was watching him. 'Don't ever use this unless you have to. You may do a lot more harm than good.'

Coll listened intently. He nodded to his uncle, turned, closed his eyes and walked through the locked door of the room.

From outside came his whoop of delight.

Gwythelyn gazed after him. 'And now we'll see,' he thought, 'whether my nephew is a wise man or a fool.'

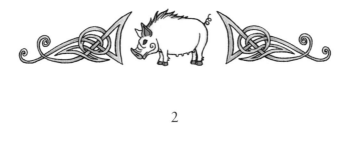

2

THE SOW

Coll travelled through the lands of the Otherworld. His abilities soon became known. He stayed at the houses of lords and kings. He could spot men disguised as animals and animals disguised as men. He was wise and clever and everyone liked him, and word got round that he knew the Great Enchantment.

One winter's morning he came to the house of Dallwyr Blindhead.

The gatekeeper said, 'Who are you and what can you do?'

'My name is Coll ap Collfrewi and I can do whatever your lord wants.'

The gatekeeper snorted. 'I doubt that. He's looking

for someone to guard his sow. No one else has dared to do it. Everyone else has run away.'

Coll stared. 'A sow? One ordinary pig?'

'Henwen is no ordinary pig.'

'I could manage her.'

The gatekeeper grinned. 'Well then, you'd better go in, hadn't you?'

Coll entered the hall and stood before Dallwyr Blindhead.

He had never been in such a scary place before. The hall was pitch black. All the windows were shuttered and there were no lights or candles. He couldn't see a thing. This was the court of the blind.

A voice came from the high seat. 'Are you Coll?'

Coll stared into the dark. He just made out a shadow dressed in dark furs. He saw a face that turned to him. He saw the glitter of steel swords stuck in the ground like a fence of war.

'I am.'

'Are you a wise man or a fool?'

Coll shrugged. 'We'll soon find out.'

Dallwyr sighed. 'I need a good man. They say you know the Great Enchantment.'

'That's true.'

'Then you'll need it. I need someone to guard Henwen, the Old White One. Wherever she goes, you have to stay with her. Over mountains, under seas, into the sky, under the earth. Above all, you have to deal with her children. Because the sow is pregnant, and all the druids say she will give birth to three good things and three terrible things. Can you do it?'

Coll nodded. 'I'll do it.'

Dallwyr Blindhead did not look convinced. But his pale face nodded. 'Then hurry. Because I think she's restless, and the time is almost come.'

Coll turned and went out of the dark hall. The sunlight was warm on his face, and for a moment it almost dazzled him. He walked round the corner of the building, and saw Henwen.

She was lying in the corner of a sty, and she was enormous.

Her skin was white as clouds, without any spot or stain. Her snout was red; her eyes were red; one of her ears was red. Her body was swollen; her glare was ferocious.

She said, 'Who are you, little scrawny boy?'

Coll folded his arms. 'I'm your keeper, Old One.'

'You'll never keep up with me.' Henwen snorted. She staggered to her feet, and the ground shook under her weight. She barged at the fence and the wood splintered. Coll jumped back.

'I'm leaving,' she snapped. 'Come if you can.'

Henwen was big and heavy but she ran like the wind. Before Coll could move she was gone, a white speck on the road. He stared in astonishment.

The gatekeeper held open the gate. 'Better hurry, magician.'

Coll took a deep breath. Then he turned himself into a hound and streaked after her. It took three miles to catch her and he came up to her just as she burst out of the Otherworld into the Island of Britain. She stopped to look at the view and Coll magicked himself back to his own shape and doubled up, panting for breath. 'Where are we?' he gasped.

Henwen rooted up a mouthful of acorns and chomped them. Saliva dribbled down her chops.

'This is Arthur's Kingdom. They call it the Island of the Mighty. We'll see how mighty they are when I've finished with them.'

Coll looked round. He saw a vast river shining under the sun. On the other side was a green land with grey mountains in the far distance.

Henwen gave him a sly look. 'Can you swim?' she asked.

And she was off. But this time Coll was ready. He grabbed her by the bristles and hung on.

With a mighty rush, Henwen plunged into the river. The current was strong, but she was stronger.

The splash of her swimming legs churned up the water. The tide turned and backed off. Thousands of birds flew away.

Coll clung tight. He was hauled through the waves, battered by the brine. He swallowed pints of water, spat it out. He couldn't see, couldn't breathe, couldn't speak.

And then he was splodging in deep mud; and then they were on land, and the sow was running.

But Coll called on all his magic and he breathed a spell of holding, so that his hand was firm on her bristles no matter what. They entered Wales and raced over fields and flat moors, through meadows riven with reens.

After an hour they came to a meadow between two sloping hills. Henwen stopped so suddenly Coll almost went flying over her shoulder. She skidded her hooves into the soil and sat down.

'Here come the first of my children,' she said.

She gave birth to twins. But they weren't cute little piglets. One was an ear of wheat and the other was a black and golden bumble bee.

'Easy to deal with,' Coll thought.

He took the ear of wheat and sowed it quickly in the field. Immediately it grew, filling the field and the next and the next with glorious waving crops. Then he made a hive for the bee from woven straw. Soon there were bees buzzing everywhere.

'This place will be called Maes y Gwenith,' Henwen said. 'Wheat Field, in Gwent Iscoed. And my gift to it is that it will have the best wheat and bees in the world.'

She set off again. She raced over the hills and along the coast into the west, bumping Coll over hedges and hills, through forest and fenland. Showers of rain came down and soaked him. The sun came out and scorched him. He hung on tight till he thought he couldn't hold on any more. Just then they came to a beautiful river valley, and the sow sat down so abruptly that this time he really did go flying over her shoulder.

He landed with a gasp and scrambled up.

'Here comes the next birth,' Henwen grinned.

She grunted and groaned. From her fuss Coll was expecting something huge. But all that lay on the ground was a tiny barley seed.

'Easy to deal with,' Coll thought.

He grabbed the barley seed and sowed it quickly in the rich brown soil. Immediately it grew, filling the valley with yellow acres of barley, all ready to cut and brew and be made into frothy beer.

'This place is called Llonion,' Henwen announced.

'And from now on they'll have the best barley in the world.'

Coll looked around and grinned. 'Well we've certainly brightened the place up.'

'You think this is easy,' Henwen said.

'It has been so far. No problem at all.'

She snorted. 'I hope your uncle taught you a lot more magic, scrawny boy. Because now we're going north, where the land is rocky and rises to the mountains. You'll never keep up. And I can feel real trouble stirring inside me.'

She set off so fast Coll only just had time to grab her before he was whisked off his feet.

Henwen ran over hills and up into the mountains. She thundered through forests. Her hooves ploughed up valleys. Her bristles gouged out cwms and lakes. She made a smashing, trampling, thundering rush into the heart of Wales.

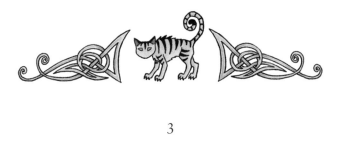

3

The Cat

Far away, in Arthur's court at Celliwic, they heard the noise.

The bards stopped singing and the servants stopped bringing the feast. Everyone stared around and listened.

'What's that?' Arthur said.

'Trouble,' Cai muttered.

Arthur nodded. 'Sounds like something's going on somewhere. Sounds like a giant or a dragon trampling up the land. Sounds like a whirlwind raging out of the sea.' He turned to his court full of marvellous men. 'Where's Clust!'

The call went out for Clust and he came. Now Clust was a little man but he had big ears. In fact Clust's hearing was so sharp that he claimed that even if he was buried seven fathoms deep in the earth he'd still be able to hear an ant fifty miles away getting out of its bed in the morning.

Arthur said, 'What can you hear?'

Clust listened. 'Big trouble, lord. I can hear a magic animal.'

'A dragon?' Cai asked.

'No. A sow. A great white sow, the Old White One herself. She's trampling all over Wales. She's reached the north and she's about to give birth to a whole heap of trouble.'

Arthur leapt up. 'Is there anyone guarding her?'

'A magician. He's hanging on as tight as he can. But we'd better get there fast.'

Arthur called for his horse Llamrei and his sword Caliburn and his dog Caball. He called his marvellous men, and they all came running, riding, leaping. And they set off in great haste towards the north.

Meanwhile, Henwen ran through snow and tempest. Coll was bumped over rocks till his teeth rattled. He was dragged through rivers of ice and over cliffs of stone. Henwen leapt over mountain passes and hurtled through caves and caverns.

When she came to the top of a hill high among the mountains she stopped so fast that Coll smacked right into her and let go of her bristles.

He almost tumbled down the slope but managed to grab a bramble and pull himself back up, hand over hand. When he got to the top Henwen grinned at him with her red snout. 'Another pair of twins.'

Coll went white. Because there on the ground, snarling at him, was a wolf cub with sharp teeth. And next to it, already flapping its wings, an eagle with cold blue eyes.

Coll moved fast. He grabbed the cub before it could run. Then he snatched the eagle. One pecked him and the other scrammed him. One clawed him and the other bit him. One scratched him and the other screamed at him.

He could barely hold them.

Henwen looked proud. 'Not so easy now, is it?' she said. 'This is the Hill of Cyferthwch and this place will have the best wolves and eagles in the world.' Then she chomped a mouthful of thistles and said, 'And you'll never keep up with me with those two in your arms.'

Coll looked round in fear. Only bleak mountains surrounded him. Then he saw two men down on the slopes, riding by as if they were going to hunt.

'Hey!' he yelled. 'Hey, you.'

The men looked up and saw him. Coll ran. He raced down to the men and dumped the wolf cub on one and the eagle in the other's hands. 'There,' he said. 'Keep them! Guard them! I've got to go!'

The men were called Brennach and Menwaedd. Brennach said, 'Fantastic! I've always wanted a wolf. I can teach it to hunt.'

Menwaedd said, 'I've always wanted an eagle. I can teach it to hunt. By the way, is that your sow? Only she's running away.'

Coll turned and gave a screech. Henwen was a speck on the next mountain.

He raced after her. He magicked himself into a fox and a swallow. He swooped down on Henwen and grabbed her and hung on, and they rampaged higher and higher into the hills, until they came to the top of Wales and looked down at the sea.

Like a green gem in the water was the Island of Mona. But leaning out of the dark mountainside like a broken tooth was a single stone.

The Black Stone.

The wind howled around it.

Snow lashed against it.

It was a lonely, desolate place.

Henwen stopped. She dug her hooves in and she crouched. She squirmed and she shivered. She said: 'This is my last child. This one will be famous throughout Wales.' She screamed and roared so much that Coll was terrified. He expected a monster,

a huge dragon, a beast of terror, and hid behind the Black Stone to watch.

But then suddenly, she gave birth.

To a kitten.

A striped, speckled, tiny, furry kitten.

'Cute,' Coll whispered.

Henwen only laughed. 'Don't be fooled, scrawny boy,' she said quietly. 'This one is a bad little beast.'

The kitten opened its mouth and gave a small mew.

And Coll saw the sharp teeth in its mouth. He saw the tiny soft claws on its paws. He saw the green, black-slitted eyes in its head.

And he knew this was the most dangerous monster he had ever seen.

He picked up the kitten.

'What are you doing?' Henwen said.

'I'm going to kill it.'

'No you're not. It's too late.'

And she was right, because already the kitten was growing. It was getting bigger and bigger in his hands. It mewed and then it hissed and then it growled. It was getting heavier second by second.

Coll ran. He didn't wait. He raced down the mountain with the kitten under one arm, and as fast as he ran the kitten grew, so that he knew he wouldn't make it to the shore before it would tear him apart. So he stopped and he whispered a word of magic.

With its strength he threw the kitten.

High into the air it flew, right over the heads of Arthur and all his men who were watching on the shore, high over the waves and out into the waters of the Menai.

The kitten landed with an enormous scream and a splash that soaked them all.

It sank under the sea, and was gone.

Coll gasped for breath. He bent double, hands on knees.

Henwen came down and stood beside him and she said, 'Easy?'

'Difficult,' Coll gasped. 'Very, very difficult.'

Henwen tore up a mouthful of gorse and chewed it. 'I'm hungry,' she said. 'It's time I was home. They'll be filling my trough up with scraps. You'd better get me there if you want your reward from Dallwyr Blindhead.'

So Coll and the sow started the long walk home.

Arthur's men looked at the ripples in the water.

'No monsters then,' Arthur said.

Cai frowned. 'I'm not so sure,' he muttered.

Coll walked wearily into his uncle's hall and Gwythelyn looked down at him from his high seat.

'So, Coll, what have you done with the magic I taught you?'

Coll shrugged. He was worn out and weary. 'I've been dragged all over Wales. I've sown wheat and barley and bees. I've given away wolves and eagles. I've killed a terrible monster. I will always be known as one of the Three Powerful Swineherds of the Island of Britain. That's what I've done.'

Gwythelyn snorted. 'Yes, but have you found out if you're a wise man or a fool?'

Coll thought about it. 'I think that will take a longer journey,' he said.

4

THE SONS OF PALUG

'Seaweed.'

'Shells.'

'Someone's stinky old boot.'

The three Sons of Palug scrambled along the shingly shore.

It was a cold wet day on the isle of Môn, and they were looking for treasure, but all they could find were washed-up scatters of worthless rubbish.

The three Sons were identical. No one could tell them apart. Their hair was red and their eyes were red. Their coats were red and their faces were reddest of all. However wild the weather, they came out every day and scrounged and scavenged whatever the sea threw up from shipwrecks or drowned castles or kingdoms under the waves.

One day they were sure they would find treasure – gold, or diamonds, or silver swords. One day, and – you never know – it might be today.

'Bladderweed.'

'A broken bucket.'

'Bits of a blackbird's nest.'

Their sack was empty. Cold winds swept the beach, and across the water the mountains of the Island of the Mighty rose like snowy peaks in a dream of winter.

A small furrow arrowed through the water towards them.

'Conkers.'

'A cracked cup without a handle.'

'A kitten.'

The eldest and middle Sons looked up. 'What?'

Youngest was looking out to sea, shading his gaze from the eye-watering wind. 'A kitten. Isn't it? Out there. Look.'

And they saw it. It was swimming ashore, a speckled, snarly kitten, its head high out of the water. As it reached the beach and ran out of the waves they saw how it shivered and shook and stood there soaked, all its fur streaming and flat.

'Oh, cute!'

'Sweet!'

'Cwtshy.'

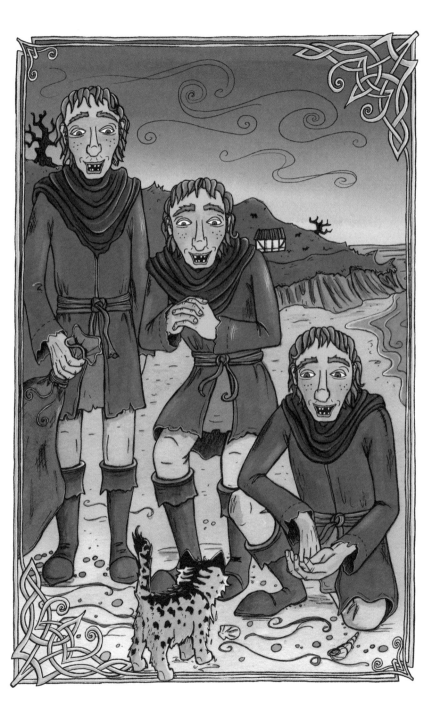

Like a row of rusty scarecrows, the brothers crouched. They grinned gappy grins and clicked their bony fingers.

'Come on then, kitty.'

'Cuteykins.'

'Puss.'

The cat watched them with its slant-green eyes. It took a step nearer and stopped and began to wash its face and whiskers. Its teeth were long and sharp, and its claws gleamed.

'Come home with us.'

'We'll play with you.'

'We'll feed you lovely food.'

The kitten stood. It walked towards them over the shingle, tail upright. It smiled a calm smile. It purred as if something oily rippled deep in its throat.

The eldest brother picked it up with an effort. 'It's so heavy.'

'We'll adopt it,' the second said.

'We'll take it home,' the third grinned. 'It can catch mice for us.'

Over the sand dunes the kitten could see the buildings of the brothers' farm. It could see barns and cowsheds. It could see sheep, cattle, goats, chickens, a growly dog.

The kitten purred a little louder.

And licked its lips.

A few weeks later, Arthur was playing chess with Cai when the gate-keeper came into the hall and said there were three beggars outside asking to see him.

'I haven't got time now. Give them some food and send them home.' Arthur lifted a chess piece and edged it forward a few squares.

Cai grinned. 'Bad move.'

The gate-keeper said, 'But look, lord, these men are desperate. They call themselves the Sons of Palug, and they're from Môn. They're gabbling about some terrible monster on the island.'

Arthur sighed. He looked at Cai. 'We'd better let them in.'

Cai moved a pawn and sat back. 'I knew this would happen. Just when I was winning.' He looked towards the door. All Arthur's men stopped talking and cleaning their weapons and looked too.

They saw three red-haired scarecrows stagger into the hall. They were as thin as sticks. Their eyes were wild and staring. They came and fell on their knees before Arthur.

'Save us from it, lord!'

'Send an army to destroy it!'

'Send a champion to kill it!'

Arthur said, 'Save you from what? And just one of you answer me. I don't want three echoes.'

The eldest Son of Palug stood up, helped by his brothers. He said, 'Lord, there's this monster. This sea-cat. We found it on the shore and took it to our farm. What a mistake! First it ate the mice. Then the rats. After that it ate the chickens, the goats, the sheep, the cattle. We had to flee before it could eat us too.'

'A cat?'

'A monstrous ferocious cat. It's grown so huge that everyone is terrified of it. Its teeth are fangs, its claws are blades of steel. Each of its eyes is as big as a bronze cauldron; its fur is striped like a leopard's, it has muscles like a lion, and it eats everything. Warriors have attacked it, nine twenties of them. The cat defeated them all. The island of Môn has become a desert. All the people have fled to the mainland in boats and ships and coracles. It's a magical beast, lord, and if you don't destroy it soon it will swim to Wales and start terrorising everyone here too.'

Arthur leaned back in his throne. 'So, the last child of Henwen the sow still lives.' He looked round at his court. 'Do you hear, my wonderful men? We must find a champion to fight the terrible cat.'

There was silence. No one liked the sound of teeth like fangs and claws like blades of steel.

But then they all saw that Cai was standing up.

'I'll fight with Palug's Cat, brother.' He smiled, coldly. 'And I will kill it, if it doesn't kill me.'

5

Gai The Fair

Have I told you about Cai?

He was the handsomest man who rode in Arthur's court. He was Arthur's foster-brother and closest, oldest friend. He was tall and elegant and mocking and ferocious in battle.

He also had some very strange magical gifts.

When Cai was born his father looked at him and said, 'My son will have cold hands and a cold heart. He'll be stubborn. Anything he carries will become invisible. No one will endure fire and water like him.'

That all came true. And in Arthur's court there were other whispers too. That Cai could live nine nights and nine days underwater. That he could grow as tall as the tallest tree in the forest. That nothing could survive a wound from his sword. So all the warriors and women and druids and bishops agreed that Cai was the one to kill the Cat.

Now he prepared his armour and his weapons. And when they were sharpened and honed and bright, he took his shield. It was as tall as he was, and decorated with blue enamel. Cai sat down and began to polish the shield. He polished it so much that it shone like a mirror. He looked in it and saw his own face staring back. He smiled. 'Now I'm ready,' he said.

An oarsman rowed him across to the island in a small boat. Behind them, crowding the shores and hills all the court of the Island of the Mighty stood and watched. Arthur himself sat on a throne high on a hill with his best men round him and Drem to tell him what was happening. Drem had excellent eyesight. Drem could see from Cornwall when a fly got up in the morning as far away as Pictland.

If Cai was in trouble they'd be going in to help him. And all the people who had fled the island scrambled up hills and out on headlands to crane their necks and stare and pray.

Cai jumped out of the boat as soon as the prow scraped the shore. The oarsman hastily backed away into open water. He was too scared to stay, because the beach was littered with bones and flocks of crows that rose noisily. Cai crunched along the shingle, turning the bones with the toe of his boot. Goats. Sheep. Cattle. It seemed as if all the flocks of the island had been slaughtered.

The bones were splintered, chewed, cracked. Cai followed the trail of them up the beach, across the dunes, into the fields. There he looked round.

The island of Môn was silent. No birds sang. No lambs bleated. A cold wind whistled over the abandoned fields. Everything was deserted.

He walked until he came to a wide grove of oak trees and there he stopped.

In the middle was an enormous pile of treasure – shields, swords, cups, furs, jewels. It was as if everything valuable on the island had been dragged out of the houses and piled up here. Cai took one step towards it.

A growl.

He turned quickly.

The Cat roared from the trees and leapt straight at him. He only just managed to drop and roll and scramble up, snatching out his sword and flinging up his shield onto his back, as the Cat landed and sprang round, spitting. Breathless, he stared at it.

The Sons of Palug had been right.

The kitten had become a green-eyed, steel-striped, iron-clawed monster. It opened its mouth and

howled, and he saw the great fangs hung with strips of flesh.

Cai closed his hand on his sword. 'Come on,' he growled. 'You tiny little thing. You don't scare me.'

The Cat snarled. Its tail swished. Then it struck. One great claw smashed down. Cai jumped aside; the claw slashed four trenches in the earth as deep as ditches. The ground shook.

'Not even close.'

Then Cai began his magic. He grew as tall as an oak. But the Cat was ready for that; it swelled like a lion and hurled itself at him. This time its hot breath seared him and his sword slashed only the tips of its iron whiskers.

Instantly he was normal size; he grabbed a branch from an oak tree and it burst into flames in his hands. He thrust it at the Cat, turning in a circle. The cat yowled and clawed and ran desperately at him.

'Cute little kitten,' Cai gasped. 'You don't really call this fighting, do you?'

The Cat roared with anger. It sprang at him, and its great paws slashed the burning branch out of his hand. Cai yelled and twisted, but this time the talons tore a wound under the armoured coat he wore. Blood dripped on the ground.

'Now that does make me a little bit cross,' Cai muttered.

He took a step backwards, and then another, the Cat pacing after him, its belly flat to the ground. He wondered why it didn't attack. One pace back, then another.

And then he felt the seawater lapping round his ankles.

'What's happening?' Arthur said nervously.

Drem looked scared. 'Cai's in the water.'

Arthur nodded. 'That's all right. No one can fight in water like Cai.'

It was true. Deep under the waves Cai walked and the Cat followed him, and even when the waves closed over Cai he still fought with a mocking grin. The Cat slashed and spat; Cai's sword flashed like lightning.

And this time he sliced a pattern of hairs from the Cat's tail and back.

It howled. It fled out of the water and Cai ran after it, back up onto the beach.

There it turned and faced him.

There was nowhere to run. There was nowhere to hide.

Cai knew this was the last attack. So he took the polished shield from his arm and held it up.

'I'm waiting,' he hissed.

6

The Polished Shield

The Cat roared in.

Its weight flattened him. Its hot breath stank of fish. Its claws raked at him.

Cai fought hard, his sword slashing, but the fur of the Cat was thick and tough; its eyes blazed with green fire. It tore off his helmet with one swipe. It opened its huge mouth to savage his throat.

Desperately he wriggled one arm free and lifted up the shield.

The sunlight caught it.

It glittered like glass.

The Cat's eyes widened in amazement.

It saw another cat.

At once its attention was fixed. It growled and the strange cat growled. It struck and the strange cat struck. Furious, the Cat clawed and snarled at its

distorted reflection in the polished metal shield. It had forgotten all about Cai. He scrambled silently up behind it and lifted his sword.

He struck once, a slice into its neck that seemed only a scratch. But a wound from Cai's sword could never be healed.

The Cat gave a yelp. It turned and stared at him. He saw the green flame in its eyes turn from anger to astonishment to fear. And then, even as it stared, the flame went out, and the Cat fell with a crash, and the whole island shook with its passing.

Cai breathed out a weary sigh. He was sore and tired and bleeding. Looking up, he saw that Arthur's men were already sailing across the Menai, coming in ships and boats and coracles. As he turned and gazed down again at the great sprawled body of the monster, he heard voices.

To his astonishment, up on the hill behind him, a small dwarfish man in a golden chariot was arguing with the boy at his side.

Cai walked over. 'You must be from the Otherworld.'

'We are. And I'm sorry,' Gwythelyn said sharply, 'that you had all this trouble. My nephew was supposed to make sure all the Sow's children were properly dealt with.'

Cai looked at Coll. 'Well they are now.'

Coll nodded. 'Maybe a wise man is someone who realises he can't do everything on his own, Uncle.'

Gwythelyn laughed. 'Maybe he is.'

Together, they watched Arthur lead the men and women of the Island of the Mighty back to their farms and fields.

About the Author

Award-winning poet and novelist Catherine Fisher was born in Newport. She has worked as a teacher, an archaeologist and as a lecturer in creative writing. These days she's a full-time writer with an international reputation, and has published many stories for young people and adults, specialising in history, myth and magic. In October 2011, she was chosen to be the very first Young People's Laureate for Wales.

Catherine's previous publications with Pont include *The Weather Dress*, a picture book for younger children, *The Hare and Other Stories*, a collection for older readers, and contributions to *Dragon Days* and *A Child's Book of Poems: All Through the Year*.

Catherine's award-winning novel *Incarceron* was chosen as The Times Book of the Year.